U0022390

First published in 2000 by Allen & Unwin Pty Ltd., Australia

大喜說故事系列

Tashi and the MAGIC FLUTE

大喜與魔笛

Anna Fienberg
Barbara Fienberg 著

Kim Gamble 繪

柯美玲 譯

三民書局

'Dad,' said Jack, 'can I ask you something?'

'Sure,' said Dad. 'What's it about—**turbo engines**, shooting stars, **hermit crabs**—I'm good at all those subjects!'

「老爸，」傑克說，「我可不可以問你一個問題？」

「好啊，」老爸說。「什麼問題？是渦輪式引擎、流星，還是寄居蟹？我可是這些方面的專家呢！」

turbo [`tɝbo] 名 渦輪

engine [`ɛndʒɪn] 名 引擎

hermit crab 寄居蟹

'No,' Jack said, 'it's like this. Say your friend is in trouble, but when you go to save him, you hurt the person who got him into trouble. Does that mean you did the wrong thing?'
'Which friend is that, Jack?' said Dad. 'Would it be my mate Charlie over the road, or is it Henry, the one I play cards with?'

'Oh, Dad, it doesn't **matter**,' sighed Jack. 'It's the idea, see—a question of right or wrong. Or say you **owe** someone a hundred dollars and...'

「不是啦，」傑克說，「事情是這樣的。假如說你的朋友有了麻煩，當你去救他的時候，卻傷到那個害他的人。這樣算不算做壞事？」

「傑克，是哪個朋友啊？」老爸問。「是住在對面的朋友查理，還是我的牌友亨利？」

「哦，老爸，那個不重要啦，」傑克嘆了一口氣。「重要的是觀念問題，你知道的嘛，就是對錯的問題。或者如果你欠人家一百元……」

matter [`mætɚ] 動 重要

owe [o] 動 欠

'Who owes a hundred dollars?' Mom came in with three bowls and spoons.

Jack **rolled** his eyes. 'It doesn't matter who, Mom! Maybe I'd better tell you the whole story—just the way Tashi told me.'

'Oh boy, ice cream, **peaches** and a Tashi story for dessert!' Dad cried **gleefully**.

'Yes,' said Jack **sternly**. 'But listen carefully, because I'll ask you some questions at the end.'

Dad leant forward, **frowning** thoughtfully, to show how serious he could be.

「誰欠了一百元啊？」老媽端著三個碗和三支調羹走了進來。

傑克翻了翻白眼。「是誰並不重要啦，老媽！看來我還是把事情的來龍去脈告訴你們好了——就像大喜說給我聽的那樣。」

「哇，冰淇淋、桃子，還有大喜的故事當點心呢！」老爸高興地叫了起來。

「是啊，」傑克一臉嚴肅地說。「可是要注意聽哦，因為最後我會問你們一些問題。」

老爸把身子往前傾，若有所思地皺起眉頭來，一副正經八百的樣子。

roll [rol] 動 轉動

peach [pitʃ] 名 桃子

gleefully [`glifəlɪ] 副 高興地

sternly [`stɝnlɪ] 副 嚴肅地

frown [fraʊn] 動 皺眉頭

‘Well,’ began Jack, ‘back in the old country, it had been a good summer and the rice had grown well. People were looking forward to a big **harvest**, when a traveler arrived with **dreadful** news. The **locusts** were coming! In the next valley he’d seen a great **swarm** of **grasshoppers** settle on the fields in the morning, leaving not one blade of grass at the end of the day.’

「嗯，」傑克開始說起故事來，「時間要回到那個古老的鄉村，經過一整個風調雨順的夏天，田裡的稻子已經結實纍纍。大伙兒都滿心期待能有個大豐收，這時卻來了一個旅人，帶來一個可怕的消息。蝗蟲快來了！他在隔壁山谷看見一大群蝗蟲，早上停在田裡，到了黃昏飛走的時候，田裡竟然一根草也不剩。」

harvest [`hɑrvɪst] 名 收穫

dreadful [`drɛdfəl] 形 可怕的

locust [`lokəst] 名 蝗蟲

swarm [swɔrm] 名 一群

grasshopper [`græsˏhɑpɚ] 名 蝗蟲

Dad **shook** his head. '**Awful damage** they do, locusts. You can ask me anything about them, son. Anything. They're one of my best subjects.'

'Later,' Jack said. 'Well, the Baron called a meeting in the village square.'

'That **sneaky** snake!' exploded Dad. 'He **diddles** everyone out of their money, doesn't he!'

老爸搖搖頭。「蝗災是很可怕的。兒子，你可以問我任何有關蝗蟲的問題，什麼都行。這方面我也很在行。」

「待會兒吧，」傑克說。「嗯，那個大地主就在村子的廣場召開了一個會議。」

「那個陰險的壞蛋！」老爸脫口而出。「大伙兒的錢都被他騙走了，對吧！」

shake [ʃek] 動 搖動（過去式 shook [ʃuk]）

awful [ˋɔfəl] 形 可怕的

damage [ˋdæmɪdʒ] 名 損害

sneaky [ˋsnikɪ] 形 陰險的

diddle [ˋdɪdl̩] 動 欺騙

‘That’s the one,’ agreed Jack. ‘But now the Baron was very worried because he owned most of the fields, although everyone in the town worked a little vegetable **patch** or had a **share** in the village rice fields.

‘At the meeting, Tashi’s grandfather **suggested hosing** the crops with **poison** but there wasn’t time to buy it. Someone else said they should cover the fields with **sheets**, but of course there weren’t enough sheets in the whole **province** to do that. Tashi racked his brains for an idea but nothing came.

「就是他，」傑克表示贊同。「可是現在大地主非常著急，因為大部分的田都是他的，村民們頂多只耕作一小塊菜園，或只分到村裡稻田的一部分。

patch [pætʃ] 名 一塊（土地）
share [ʃɛr] 名 一份

「開會的時候，大喜的爺爺提議在農作物上灑農藥，可是現在去買農藥已經來不及了。還有人說應該用床單把田蓋住，但是整個省也湊不出那麼多的床單。大喜絞盡腦汁，卻怎麼也想不出個辦法來。

suggest [səgˋdʒɛst] 動 提議

hose [hoz] 動 澆灑

poison [ˋpɔɪzn̩] 名 毒藥

sheet [ʃit] 名 床單

province [ˋpravɪns] 名 省

‘Just when everyone was in **despair**, a stranger stepped into the middle of the square. He was a very odd-looking **fellow**, dressed in a rainbow colored shirt and silk **trousers**. On his head was a red cap with a bell. The people had to **blink** as they stared at him—he **glowed** like a flame.

‘“I can save your fields from the locusts,” he said. Tashi looked up into his eyes. They were **pale** and **hooded**.

「就在大伙兒絕望的時候，一個陌生人走到廣場中央。他長得好怪，身上穿著一件七彩的襯衫，和一條絲質的褲子，頭上戴著一頂掛著小鈴鐺的紅帽子。大伙兒看著他，眼睛都忍不住地眨呀眨的——因為他就好像火焰一樣地發亮。

despair [dɪ`spɛr] 名 絕望
fellow [`fɛlo] 名 傢伙
trousers [`traʊzɚz] 名 褲子
blink [blɪŋk] 動 眨眼睛
glow [glo] 動 發光

「『我有辦法拯救你們的稻田免於蝗災，』他說。大喜抬頭看著他的眼睛。他的眼睛半張半闔的毫無神采。

pale [pel] 形 沒有神采的
hooded [`hʊdɪd] 形 半睜半閉的

‘“Can you really? How?” the people shouted as they crowded around. They wanted to believe him, and there was something about

him, this man. You could feel a kind of power that made you think he would **deliver** whatever he **promised** to do. But his eyes were full of **shadows**.

‘“What will you need?” asked the Baron.

「『你真的有辦法？怎麼做？』大伙兒圍著他七嘴八舌地問。大家都想要相信他，而且這個人似乎真有本事。你可以感覺到有一股力量要你相信他會完成他所承諾的任何事情。可是他的眼神看起來不懷好意。

「『那你要什麼報酬？』大地主問。

deliver [dɪˋlɪvɚ] 動 履行

promise [ˋprɑmɪs] 動 答應

shadow [ˋʃædo] 名 陰影

'"Nothing except my **payment**," **replied** the stranger. "You must give me a bag of gold when the locusts have gone."

'The people quickly agreed, and it was just as well they did. Only a moment later the sky began to grow dark and a deep **thrumming** like a million fingers **drumming** could be heard.

「『只要酬金，』那個陌生男子回答。『蝗蟲走了以後，你們得給我一袋黃金。』

「大伙兒馬上就同意了，也幸好他們同意了。因為不到一會兒工夫，天空開始暗了下來，遠處傳來一陣低沈的嗡嗡聲，就好像有上百萬根手指頭同時在敲啊敲的。

payment [`pemənt] 名 酬勞

reply [rɪ`plaɪ] 動 回答

thrum [θrʌm] 動 嗡嗡作響

drum [drʌm] 動 咚咚地敲擊

‘Clouds of locusts **appeared overhead**, clouds so big and black that the sun was **blocked** completely, and then wah! just like that, the noise stopped and they settled on the village rice fields and gardens.

「成群結隊的蝗蟲出現在空中，黑壓壓的一大片，把太陽完全給遮住了，然後『嘩』的一聲！就這樣，吵雜的聲音停止了，蝗蟲全停在村子的稻田和菜園裡。

appear [ə`pɪr] 動 出現

overhead [ˌovɚ`hɛd] 副 在頭上

block [blɑk] 動 遮住

'But before the locusts could eat a blade of grass, the stranger brought out his **flute** and played a single **piercing note**. It **echoed** in the silence and the locusts **quivered**. Six shrill notes followed, and as the last note sounded, the locusts rose as one, and flew away to the south. In three minutes the air was clear.

「但是沒等蝗蟲啃掉任何一片葉子，那個陌生人就拿出他的笛子，吹出一個刺耳的單音。那笛音在寂靜中迴響，只見一隻隻蝗蟲抖動了起來。緊接著又是六個尖銳的笛音，等到最後一個音一響起，所有的蝗蟲一起飛了起來，往南方飛走了。不到三分鐘的時間，天空又明亮了起來。

flute [flut] 名 笛子
piercing [`pɪrsɪŋ] 形 刺耳的
note [not] 名 音調
echo [`ɛko] 動 迴響
quiver [`kwɪvɚ] 動 顫抖

'There was a **stunned** silence. People looked at each other, hardly able to believe what they had just seen. Tashi's grandfather ran up to the stranger and shook his hand, thanking him, but the Baron **stepped in** and **cut** him **off**. He gathered the Elders around him, saying, "Let's not be too hasty in our thanks. We can't be sure it was the stranger's flute that drove off the locusts. Maybe they would have gone **of their own accord**. And, **in any case**, a bag of gold is far too much to pay for one moment's work."

「大伙兒看得目瞪口呆，你看我、我看你的，簡直不能相信剛剛所看到的那一幕。大喜的爺爺跑上前去，握著那個陌生人的手向他道謝，大地主卻站出來打斷了他。他把眾長老聚集過去，開口說，『先別急著謝他。我們還不確定是不是陌生人的笛聲趕走了蝗蟲，也許是牠們自己要飛走的。再說，不管怎樣，才做那麼一點事情就要付給他一袋黃金，也未免太便宜他了。』

stun [stʌn] 動 使嚇呆

step in 介入

cut off 打斷

of one's own accord 主動地

in any case 不管怎樣

‘When Tashi’s father and the Elders **disagreed**, the Baron went on, “I know none of you has more than a few **silver pieces** between you, so who do you **suppose** would have to pay the most of it? Me, of course. Well, I won’t do it, and you must all **stand by** me.”

「大喜的爸爸和眾長老不同意他的看法，大地主卻繼續說，『我知道你們大家連幾塊銀幣也湊不出來，那你們認為誰得付這個錢？當然是我。而我呢，是絕對不會出這個錢的，所以你們都得站在我這一邊。』

disagree [ˌdɪsəˋgri] 動 不同意

silver piece 銀幣

suppose [səˋpoz] 動 認為

stand by 支持

‘Tashi felt a shiver of dread. This was the wrong thing to do. He could see that many of the others were unhappy too, and some of them started to **argue** with the Baron but he **brushed** them **aside**. He walked over to the stranger and **tossed** him a single gold coin, saying, “Here you are, fellow, you earned that coin easily enough.”

‘The stranger let the coin fall to the ground and slowly looked around at the people. “Do you all agree with him?”

‘The people **shuffled** and looked away.

‘“You will be sorry—oh, how very sorry,” the stranger said quietly, and he **drifted** away, the bright flame of him shimmering in the distance.

‘On the way home Tashi’s grandfather took his hand and sighed.

「大喜心頭一顫。這麼做是不對的。他看得出來其他很多人也不太高興，有些人開始和大地主吵了起來，但是大地主根本不理會他們。他走到那個陌生人面前，丟給他一枚金幣，接著說，『兄弟，這個給你，對你來說這枚金幣實在太好賺了。』

「那陌生人任由那枚金幣掉到地上，緩緩地看著周遭每一個人。『你們都同意他的做法嗎？』

「大伙兒不安地動來動去，迴避著他的眼光。

「『你們會後悔的——哦，會非常後悔的，』陌生人靜靜地說著，然後轉身離開，他身上耀眼的光芒也隨著消失在遠方。

argue [`ɑrgju] 動 爭論

brush aside 不理會

toss [tɔs] 動 扔擲

shuffle [`ʃʌfl̩] 動 不安地挪動身子

drift [drɪft] 動 移動

「回家的路上，大喜的爺爺牽著他的手，嘆了一口氣。

‘“We did a bad thing today, Tashi. We **robbed** that man of his reward.”

‘“Yes,” said Tashi, “and I have a **horrible** cold feeling in my **tummy** telling me this is not the end of it. There was something about the way the stranger looked at us when he left. He’s not an **ordinary** man, that’s for sure.”

‘Tashi’s family said that there was nothing they could do tonight but that in the morning they would speak with the Elders.

「『大喜，我們今天做錯了一件事。我們搶走了那個男人應得的賞金。』

「『是啊，』大喜說，『而且我心裡頭有一種很可怕的感覺，覺得這件事情不會就這樣結束。那個陌生人臨走前看我們的眼光好詭異。可以肯定的是，他絕對不是一個普通人。』

「大喜的家人說今晚他們也無計可施，但等明天天一亮，他們就去找長老們商量。

rob [rɑb] 動 搶奪

horrible [ˋhɔrəbl̩] 形 可怕的

tummy [ˋtʌmɪ] 名 肚子

ordinary [ˋɔrdəˏnɛrɪ] 動 普通的

They would find the stranger and promise to pay him, a little at a time.

'Tashi was too **restless** and worried to sleep. Finally he jumped out of bed and went off to see if Wise-as-an-Owl had returned yet. He had been visiting his Younger Sister who lived in the next village. Surely he would have some good **advice**.

他們要找到那個陌生人，答應把錢付給他，一次付一點。

「大喜擔心得睡不著覺。最後，他跳下床，出門去看看聰明道人回來了沒有。聰明道人去拜訪住在隔壁村子的妹妹。他一定會給一些好建議的。

restless [`rɛstlɪs] 形 不安的

advice [əd`vaɪs] 名 建議

'And that is why Tashi, alone of all the children in the village, never heard those first beautiful, **magical** notes from the stranger's flute. The children sat up in bed and listened. They **ached** to hear more. And soon it seemed that their **veins** ran with golden music, not blood, and they had to follow those notes to stay **alive**. Quietly they **slipped** from their houses and followed the music, out of the town, across the fields and into the forest.

'Next morning there were **screams** and cries as parents discovered that their children were missing.

'"I knew it! I knew it!" Tashi cried as he ran back into the village. Just then he **spied** some pumpkin **seeds** on the road. Hai Ping! Tashi's friend Hai Ping **nibbled** them all the time, and what's more he'd had a hole in his **pocket** lately so that he left a trail of seeds wherever he went. Without a word Tashi set off, out of the town, across the fields and into the forest.

「大喜就是因為這樣，才沒有和村子裡其他小孩一樣，聽到陌生人吹奏的美妙、 神奇的笛音。那些孩子全都從床上坐起來聽。他們很想再多聽一些。不久，在他們的血管裡流動的似乎變成了曼妙的樂音，而不是血液，而只有跟隨那笛音才能活命。於是他們一個個悄悄地溜出了家門，隨著笛音走出村子、越過田野、進入了森林。

magical [`mædʒɪkḷ] 形 有魔力的

ache [ek] 動 急切地想做

vein [ven] 名 血管

alive [ə`laɪv] 形 活著的

slip [slɪp] 動 悄悄溜走

「隔天早上，當爸爸媽媽們發現小孩子不見的時候，尖叫聲和哭喊聲此起彼落。

「『我就知道！我就知道！』大喜一邊叫一邊跑回村子。就在這個時候，他發現路上有一些南瓜籽。海平！大喜的朋友海平老是在啃南瓜籽，最近他的口袋破了一個洞，所以他走到哪裡，南瓜籽就掉到哪裡。大喜二話不說馬上就走出村子、越過田野、走進了森林。

scream [skrim] 名 尖叫聲
spy [spaɪ] 動 發現
seed [sid] 名 種子
nibble [`nɪbl̩] 動 一點一點地吃
pocket [`pakɪt] 名 口袋

'As the darkness of the trees closed around him, Tashi heard the faint notes of the sweetest, most lovely **melody**. It was like Second Cousin's finest dark chocolate **dissovled** into air. It made his mouth water, his ears ache, his heart pump quickly. And his fears of the stranger came flooding back. Now he knew why he'd been so uneasy about the piper. There was a story his grandmother once told him about a piper and a plague of rats. Tashi bent down and **scooped** up some **clay** to **stuff** into his ears. It was the hardest thing he'd ever done. He closed his eyes as the sounds of the music and forest died away.

「當樹影籠罩著大喜的時候，他聽到遠處隱隱約約傳來最甜美、最迷人的旋律。那樂音就好像二表哥最好的黑巧克力溶化在空氣中一樣，讓他開始流口水、耳朵發疼、心跳加速。這時候大喜對那個陌生人的恐懼又湧上了心頭。現在，他終於明白為什麼那個吹笛人令他如此不安了。他奶奶曾告訴過他一個有關吹笛人和鼠疫的故事。大喜彎下身子，抓起一把泥土塞住耳朵。長這麼大就數這件事最困難。然後他閉上眼睛，那樂音和森林裡的聲音逐漸消失。

melody [`mɛlədɪ] 名 旋律
dissolve [dɪ`zalv] 動 溶化
scoop [skup] 動 挖
clay [kle] 名 泥土
stuff [stʌf] 動 塞進

'The pumpkin seeds had been getting harder to find and now they stopped altogether. But Tashi continued along the path, following **clues** he'd learned to read—a broken **twig**, a **thread** caught on a thorn **bush**. At last, through the trees, he saw two little boys. They were the smallest of the village children and were **straggling** behind. They mouthed something which Tashi couldn't hear, and pointed up ahead.

「南瓜籽越來越難找，最後連一顆也找不到了。可是大喜還是繼續循著小路上可判讀的線索往前走去——一根斷掉的小樹枝、一條被荊棘樹叢勾住的線。最後，從樹縫間他看到兩個小男孩。他們是村子裡年紀最小的孩子，正搖搖晃晃地跟在隊伍的最後面，嘴裡喃喃說著什麼，大喜也聽不見，他們的手還指著前面。

clue [klu] 名 線索

twig [twɪg] 名 樹枝

thread [θrɛd] 名 線

bush [bʊʃ] 名 樹叢

straggle [`strægl̩] 動 搖搖晃晃地走

'Tashi saw the other children nearing the top of the **hill**. Suddenly he realized where they were all heading and his blood **froze**. The path ended in a sheer drop, down, down, a hundred **meters** down to the rushing waters of a mountain **gorge**. The piper was playing the flute while the children streamed past him—towards the **cliff**. He was playing them to their deaths! Wah!

「大喜看到其他的孩子就快走到山頂了。突然，他明白了他們正要往哪裡走去，整個人都嚇僵了。那條小路的盡頭是一個一百多公尺高的斷崖，下面峽谷的水流湍急。那個吹笛人吹著笛子，孩子們則順著他的身旁走過——走向斷崖。原來他想害死他們！哇！

hill [hɪl] 名 山丘

freeze [friz] 動 凍結（過去式 froze [froz]）

meter [`mitɚ] 名 公尺

gorge [gɔrdʒ] 名 峽谷

cliff [klɪf] 名 懸崖

‘Tashi raced up and burst out of the bushes. He **butted** the piper over, **knocking** the flute out of his hands. The children stopped, their eyes no longer blank, their minds no longer **bewitched**. Slowly they gathered around as Tashi and the stranger **struggled** towards the edge of the drop.

‘“The piper was leading you over this cliff!” Tashi gasped. The children **formed** a wall and closed in on the piper.

「大喜快步跑向前，從樹叢裡衝了出來。他把吹笛人撞倒，也把他手中的笛子撞掉了。這個時候，所有的孩子都停下腳步，眼神不再空洞，頭腦也清醒過來了。他們慢慢地聚集過來，而大喜和那個陌生人則一直扭打到斷崖邊。

「『這個吹笛人正要引你們從這個斷崖跳下去呢！』大喜喘著氣說。孩子們排成一道人牆，將吹笛人團團圍住。

butt [bʌt] 動 衝撞

knock [nɑk] 動 撞擊

bewitch [bɪˋwɪtʃ] 動 使著迷

struggle [ˋstrʌgḷ] 動 扭打

form [fɔrm] 動 排成

‘With a **desperate** pull, Tashi broke free from the stranger and rolled away towards the flute, which was lying half-hidden in the grass. He picked it up and **hurled** it with all his **strength** out over the cliff edge.

「大喜用力一扯，從陌生人手中掙脫，連翻帶爬地滾到笛子旁邊，那根笛子正半掩在草堆裡。大喜撿起笛子，使盡全力丟下斷崖。

desperate [`dɛspərɪt] 形 拼命的

hurl [hɝl] 動 投擲

strength [strɛŋθ] 名 力量

'The stranger gave a **groan** of **rage** but Tashi cried, "It wasn't the children's fault that you weren't paid. You had better go quickly before our parents come."

'The stranger looked up at the **stony** faces of the children and he **shrugged**. They moved aside to let him pass and all watched silently as he **disappeared** into the forest.

「那個陌生人生氣地哼了一聲，不過大喜大聲對他說，『你沒有拿到賞金不是這些孩子的錯。在我們的爸爸媽媽來之前，你最好趕快走吧。』

「那個陌生人抬頭看著面無表情的孩子們，聳了聳肩。孩子們往旁邊一站，挪出一條路來讓他通過，接著大家就靜靜地看著他消失在森林裡。

groan [gron] 名 哼聲
rage [redʒ] 名 憤怒
stony [\`stonɪ] 形 面無表情的
shrug [ʃrʌg] 動 聳肩
disappear [ˌdɪsə\`pɪr] 動 消失

‘The children met the search party of parents on the way back to the village and they told them what had happened. Some parents **wept**, and they looked at each other with shame.

‘“Just think,” they said, “but for Tashi, we would have been too late.”

‘The Baron kept very busy away from the village for the next few weeks and when he did finally return, he looked rather **guilty** and was so polite that people thought he must be **sickening** for something. But he was soon back to tricking people out of their wages and charging too much for his **watermelons** again, so life went on as before.’

‘Blasted Baron!’ cried Dad. ‘He’s got the morals of a **dung beetle**!’

「孩子們在回村子的路上遇到前來尋找他們的父母，就把事情的來龍去脈告訴他們。有些父母哭了起來，個個滿臉羞愧地你看著我、我看著你。

「『想想看，』他們說，『要不是大喜，一切就來不及了。』

「接下來的幾個星期大地主一直在村外忙著，等到他終於回來的時候，臉上堆滿了歉意，而且變得很有禮貌，大家都以為他一定是生病了。但是過沒多久，他又恢復老樣子，開始去騙取村民的工資、哄抬西瓜的價錢，所以啦，日子又跟從前一樣了。」

「該死的大地主！」老爸大聲地罵。「簡直跟扒糞蟲一樣骯髒齷齪！」

weep [wip] 動 哭泣（過去式 wept [wɛpt]）

guilty [\`gɪltɪ] 形 內疚的

sicken [\`sɪkən] 動 生病

watermelon [\`wɑtɚ,mɛlən] 名 西瓜

dung beetle 扒糞蟲

'Worse. Dung beetles do some very good work,' put in Mom.

'But don't you see,' said Jack. 'It wasn't right that the piper never got paid—'

'But he was about to do a very dreadful thing!'

'But if he hadn't been **treated** badly **in the first place—**'

'Well,' said Mom, clearing away the dishes, 'people have been **discussing** what's right and wrong for **centuries—**and we've only got half an hour before *The Magic Pudding*'s on.'

「錯了。扒糞蟲還會做些有助益的工作呢，」老媽插了一句。

「可是你們不明白嗎？」傑克說。「沒付錢給那個吹笛人是不對的——」

「可是他竟然打算做那麼可怕的事哩！」

「可是如果他一開始沒有受到不公平的待遇——」

「嗯，」老媽一邊收拾盤子一邊說，「大家已經討論是非對錯的問題好幾個世紀了——但現在只剩半小時，『魔法布丁』就要開始演了。」

treat [trit] 動 對待

in the first place 最初

discuss [dɪˋskʌs] 動 討論

century [ˋsɛntʃərɪ] 名 世紀

'Yeah,' agreed Dad. 'Why don't you ask me about turbo engines—they don't take so long, and they take you far!'
Jack **grinned**. 'The day Tashi found a pair of magic shoes, he traveled 100 **kilometers** in one **leap**!'
'No, really?' cried Dad. Then his face dropped. 'But I bet that's another story, right?'
'Right,' laughed Jack. 'And now, Dad, the clock's **ticking**. What would you have done if *you* were the piper?'

「說的也是，」老爸表示贊同。「你要不要問我渦輪式引擎的問題——他們不用花很多時間回答，還可以帶你到很遠的地方去呢！」

傑克笑一笑。「有一天大喜發現了一雙魔鞋，他一跳就跳了一百公里呢！」

「不會吧，真的嗎？」老爸大叫了起來。然後他臉一沈。「我猜那又是另外一個故事，對吧？」

「沒錯，」傑克哈哈大笑。「老爸，現在開始計時。如果你是那個吹笛人，你會怎麼做？」

grin [grɪn] 動 露齒而笑
kilometer [kɪ`lɑmɪtɚ] 名 公里
leap [lip] 名 跳
tick [tɪk] 動 發出滴答聲

大喜說故事系列

探索英文叢書・中高級　中英對照，每本均附CD

全新的大喜故事來囉！
這回大喜又將碰上什麼樣的難題呢？
讓我們趕快來瞧瞧！

Anna Fienberg & Barbara Fienberg／著
Kim Gamble／繪　王盟雄／譯

大喜與寶鞋

大喜的表妹阿蓮失蹤了！
為了尋找阿蓮，
大喜穿上了飛天的寶鞋。
寶鞋究竟會帶他到哪裡去呢？

大喜與算命仙

大喜就要死翹翹了！？
這可不妙！
盧半仙提議的方法，
真的救得了大喜嗎？

國家圖書館出版品預行編目資料

大喜與魔笛 / Anna Fienberg,Barbara Fienberg著;Kim Gamble繪;柯美玲譯.－－初版一刷.－－臺北市;三民，民91
面;公分--(探索英文叢書.大喜說故事系列;14)
中英對照
ISBN 957-14-3624-0 (平裝)
1.英國語言一讀本

805.18

© 大喜與魔笛

著作人 Anna Fienberg Barbara Fienberg
繪 圖 Kim Gamble
譯 者 柯美玲
發行人 劉振強
著作財產權人 三民書局股份有限公司
臺北市復興北路三八六號
發行所 三民書局股份有限公司
地址 / 臺北市復興北路三八六號
電話 / 二五〇〇六六〇〇
郵撥 / 〇〇〇九九九八——五號
印刷所 三民書局股份有限公司
門市部 復北店 / 臺北市復興北路三八六號
重南店 / 臺北市重慶南路一段六十一號
初版一刷 中華民國九十一年四月
編 號 S 85608
定 價 新臺幣壹佰柒拾元整
行政院新聞局登記證局版臺業字第〇二〇〇號

ISBN 957-14-3624-0 (平裝)

網路書店位址：http://www.sanmin.com.tw